Laurent de Brunhoff

BABAR'S
Rescue

HARRY N. ABRAMS, INC., PUBLISHERS

Babar, King of the Elephants, decided to take his youngest child, Isabelle, camping in the mountains. Celeste and the rest of the family helped load the Jeep with camping gear, fishing tackle, sleeping bags, and food.

Babar and Isabelle drove several hours from Celesteville, singing songs as they went.

At nightfall, they set up their tent and made a fire, which kept them warm. Babar told Isabelle stories about brave elephants until she fell asleep.

The next morning, they packed up their gear.

"From here we have to go on foot," said Babar.

He sent Isabelle to get water. Pretending to be an explorer, Isabelle walked far upstream until she found a waterfall. She filled two bottles with cold mountain water. She couldn't wait to show her father how well she had done her job.

When she returned to the camp, Babar was gone. Isabelle called out, "Papa! I don't like this, Papa. Please come back!" Babar did not come back, and at first Isabelle cried.

Then she sat next to the remains of the fire and thought.
She could see that some bushes were broken. Had a wild beast
been there? Had Babar been carried off against his will?

At last she said to herself, "I must rescue my father." She picked up her backpack and set off along the trail of broken bushes.

After walking for hours, she began to feel very tired. She was looking for a good place to rest when she heard a rustling in the bushes, then a roar. Out of the underbrush sprang a lion.

Isabelle took a deep breath for courage and said, "I am going to rescue my father."

"In that case," said the lion, "climb on my back and I'll help you find him."

Isabelle sat on his back, holding on to his mane and bouncing as the lion loped up the mountain. Suddenly, something flew out of the trees and landed behind her. Isabelle screamed before she saw it was only a monkey.

"I am going to rescue my father," she told him.

The monkey replied, "In that case, I will help you. I have excellent vision and can be your scout."

He told her that the mountain they were climbing was an extinct volcano. "I've heard that there's a city in the crater," he added.

"Maybe my father is in that city," said Isabelle. "We have to find a way to get there."

When it grew dark, they settled down for the night. Isabelle lay against the lion while the monkey did acrobatics to cheer her up. Soon she fell asleep.

All the next morning, they traveled through the forest. Isabelle was not afraid because she had the lion and the monkey for company.

The monkey went out scouting and came back with bad news. The trail of broken bushes ended at a stone wall a mile ahead. "How could that be?" Isabelle asked.

But they kept going and in the very
place where the trail disappeared,
a snake lay coiled.

"I am going to rescue my father," Isabelle said
bravely. "But the trail ends right where you're sitting."

The snake replied, "In that case, I will help you. I
know how to make the mountain open."

He wrapped himself around a little sapling and pulled until it lay flat on the ground. A door hidden in the rock swung open, revealing a tunnel.

"Follow that," he said, "to the city in the crater. But only the monkey and I can go with you. The lion would be too noticeable."

In the tunnel, the monkey and the snake kept up a constant stream of conversation so the little elephant would not be afraid. But Isabelle was not afraid. The tunnel was not too dark, since some old-fashioned lamps lit the way. And although the ground was wet, it felt nice and cool to Isabelle after her ride through the brush.

At the end of the tunnel, an amazing sight greeted Isabelle. A beautiful city was built inside the crater, with stairs and cable cars leading to the heights.

The inhabitants seemed to be elephants, but their ears were striped and they were dressed in togas. Some carried lyres, which they stroked now and then to produce lovely music.

To walk among them unnoticed, Isabelle saw that she had to have stripes. She took a marker out of her backpack and asked the monkey to draw stripes on her ears.

"With pleasure," he said. "I pride myself on my draftsmanship."

When the monkey was done, Isabelle made herself a toga out of her ground cloth. Then she looked like all the other striped elephants.

In the street, some of the striped elephants said good day to her. One of them looked at her kindly and sang a good-day song, accompanying himself on the lyre.

Coming upon an ice cream store, Isabelle realized she was hungry. She had no money, but she noticed that no one seemed to pay for the ice cream with money. Customers just sang a song, took their ice cream, and walked away. Isabelle got in line, asked for two scoops of vanilla, and sang "Happy Birthday."

The vendor was delighted. "That's the best payment I've ever received," he said. "Will you teach me that song?"

"Gladly," replied Isabelle, and she did. Then she said, "Perhaps you can tell me where I might find the elephant without stripes?"

"I'm sorry," the vendor replied, "but I'm not important enough to know where he is being held."

Isabelle shivered. So her father was a prisoner!

Isabelle wandered through the city for many hours looking for her father. Where were they keeping him? She and the monkey were sitting on a bench in the center of town when she noticed a flagpole.

"Climb to the top," she said, "and see if you find something that looks like a prison."

The monkey was soon back with his report: "There's a flat grassy terrace on the side of the crater."

"I see an unstriped elephant who looks stuck there." "That must be the place," said Isabelle. "We'll wait until dark, then climb up to it."

That night, with the snake's help, Isabelle and the monkey climbed up the side of the crater until they reached the terrace.

There was Babar, asleep in a hammock.
"Papa," Isabelle whispered. "Wake up! It's Isabelle. I've come to rescue you."

Babar woke up. He smiled when he saw his daughter. "I'm glad you're here," he said. "I was worried about you. Now I can relax completely."

"What are you talking about?" said Isabelle. "We have to get out of here, back to Celesteville."

"What for?" said Babar. "It's very pleasant here, and the striped elephants treat me with the greatest courtesy. Their music is enchanting, their food is delicious, and they only want me to tell them stories. Why should I leave?"

"But you are the King of the Elephants in Celesteville!" exclaimed Isabelle.

"Let someone else be king," said Babar, and he fell back asleep.

Isabelle was stunned. What had they done to her father?

In the morning, a delegation of striped elephants came by cable car up to the terrace to visit Babar. A magnificent chorus stood before him and sang a song to greet the new day.

Isabelle stayed hidden. As she watched, a striped elephant brought Babar a pitcher of watermelon smoothie. Isabelle saw him put some powder into the glass.

"Drink, King of the Unstriped Elephants," he said. "Later, you will tell us more stories about your people and their city." Then the chorus went away.

Isabelle knew what she had to do. She knocked the glass over, pretending it was an accident. Then she refilled it from the pitcher, giving her father some unpoisoned smoothie to drink.

Several hours later, Babar looked around as though he had just woken up. "What am I doing here?" he asked. "What happened to your ears, Isabelle?"

She told him about the secret door and the poisoned smoothie, and how the lion, the monkey, and the snake had helped her.

"I will pretend for today that nothing has changed," Babar said, "and tonight we will escape. Send the monkey to tell the lion to keep the door open."

Isabelle was glad to have her father back again.

When the striped elephants came for their story hour that afternoon, they brought Babar another watermelon smoothie. But this time he did not drink it.

When the sun went down, Babar and Isabelle unraveled the hammock to make a rope and climbed down to the city.

They made their way through the deserted streets to the entrance of the tunnel.

Then they hurried through the tunnel and out the secret
door to where the lion and the monkey were waiting.

As they hiked back to the Jeep, Babar kept looking over his shoulder. But no one followed them.

Home in Celesteville, he called all the citizens together and told them what had happened. He gave Isabelle a medal and certificates of honor to the lion, the snake, and the monkey.

"This adventure showed how brave and resourceful my little girl is," said Babar, "and I am proud of her for rescuing me. Nevertheless I hope she never has to rescue me again!"

The entire audience cheered loudly in reply, but no one cheered louder than Isabelle.

Library of Congress Cataloging-in-Publication-Data

Brunhoff, Laurent de, 1925–
Babar's Rescue / Laurent de Brunhoff.
p. cm.
Summary: When Babar and Isabelle go on a camping trip,
the king is captured by mysterious striped elephants
and it is up to Isabelle, with the help of a monkey,
a lion, and a snake, to rescue him.

ISBN 0-8109-4839-7
[1. Elephants—Fiction. 2. Kidnapping—Fiction. 3. Camping—Fiction. 4. Animals—Fiction.] . Title.

PZ7.B82843Bah 2004
[E]—dc22

2003013239

Illustrations copyright © 1993, 2004 Laurent de Brunhoff
Text copyright © 1993, 2004 Phyllis Rose de Brunhoff

Printed and bound in China

10 9 8 7 6 5 4 3 2 1

Harry N. Abrams, Inc.
100 Fifth Avenue
New York, N.Y. 10011
www.abramsbooks.com

Abrams is a subsidiary of
LA MARTINIÈRE
G R O U P E